Happy Birthday Emma!

This book was made especially for
Emma!
Happy Birthday!

Happy Birthday, Emma,
it is such a special day!

You're going to have a party,
where the kids can play and play.

Your friends will come
to celebrate...

They'll have a lot of fun!

They'll play some games,

and have some cake,

and skip, and jump, and run!

Today's your birthday, Emma,

You might play out on the slide!

Or maybe a nice puppet show,
if you all stay inside!

They'll bring balloons,
and presents...

And there might just be a clown!

And some of your good buddies
will be jumping up and down!

Maybe you will go outside,
and play with all your friends.

The day will be your special day,
from morning till it ends.

So, Happy, Happy Birthday!

To a girl who's really sweet!

A girl that's super-special...

from her head
down to her feet!

Happy Birthday Emma!

Sally was born in Jackson, Michigan. She has lived all over the country with her husband,
Fred. They have 3 grown children, and they all live in Louisville, KY. She has written over
30 children's books and had her first book published in 2000. Sneaky Snail Stories are all
sweet and simple rhyming books with really cute illustrations. You can see all the Sneaky
Snail Stories at: www.sneakysnailstories.com
Other books by Sally:

No Pancakes for Puppy
Grandma and Grandpa Love You
Your Aunt Loves You
The Best Day

Emma's Hilarious Horse Book (personalized for boys or girls with cats, dogs, penguins or
frogs)
Emma, the Super, Amazing, Awesome, Intelligent, Girly-Girl (personalized)
Noah the Basketball Star (personalized for several sports for boys or girls)
Noah's Very Own Cook Book (personalized for boys or girls)
Grandma and Grandpa Love Emma (personalized from any relative for boys or girls)
Emma Turns One! (personalized for boys or girls ages 1-6)   and many more....

website: www.sneakysnailstories.com   facebook: Sneaky Snail Stories
Etsy: (search for) thesneakysnailstore   Amazon: (search for) Sally Helmick North

see all the Sneaky Snail Stories at www.sneakysnailstories.com

74799639R00015

Made in the USA
Columbia, SC
06 August 2017